ONE OCTOBER . . .

1

THUMP! THUMP! THUMP!

BRUSHA! BRUSHA!

RRRRRRRRR!

DIGADIGADIGADIGADIGA!

HALLOWEEN, HALLOWEEN, HALLOWEEN!

MOM! DID YOU GET THE DEFENDER COSTUME?

GOOD MORNING, ANDREW!

OH, SWEETIE... I WENT TO EVERY SINGLE STORE LAST NIGHT AND THEY WERE *ALL* SOLD OUT.

YOU DIDN'T GET IT?!

WHAT AM I GONNA WEAR AT *SCHOOL?!*

DON'T WORRY...

I *MADE* YOU A DEFENDER COSTUME INSTEAD!

YOU *MADE* ONE?

BUT, UH, IT DOESN'T LOOK, UM...

I EVEN DUG UP MY GRANDPA'S WORLD WAR II GOGGLES AND SOME LONG UNDERWEAR!

NOW YOU'LL LOOK JUST LIKE DEFENDER!

THANKS, MOM!

WONDER IF IT'S TOO LATE TO PRETEND I'M SICK?

IV

AFTER SCHOOL.

V

MUCH LATER.

GOOD HAUL TONIGHT! IF I HEAD HOME NOW, I MIGHT STILL CATCH THE DEFENDER HALLOWEEN SPECIAL ON TV!

UH-OH...

WIMP TAX! COST IS ONE BAG OF CANDY!

NO FAIR! YOU CAN'T HAVE MY CANDY— I EARNED IT! GET YOUR OWN CANDY, GARETH!

THE WHINER TAX IS A MOUTHFUL OF MY FIST!

HERE, HAVE ALL MY CANDY! HOPE YOU LIKE IT!

WHAT A JERK! I'D LIKE TO KNOCK GARETH AROUND— SEE HOW HE FEELS!

HMM. WHAT WOULD DEFENDER DO?

VIII

DUDE . . . ?

WHOA! I'M SWINGING BACK! GOTTA STOP MYSELF!

COME TO *PAPA*, NERD!

≈HUNFF!≈

SMACK!

≈OOF!≈

HEY, LOOKIT! I GOT *HIS* CANDY, TOO!

THWACK!

BAM!

WHUD!

BIFF!!

NICE JOB, SPARROWHAWK! I COULDN'T HAVE DONE IT WITHOUT YOU, CHUM!

WELL, I LEARNED FROM THE *BEST!* NOW LET'S GO FIND THE *MAGUS!*

WE'LL TAKE THE FIGHT TO HIS—

LOOK OUT!

WHEN DID THE BOSTON TEA PARTY TAKE PLACE?

AT RECESS.

I GOT IT! I GOT IT! I—

SMOOTH MOVE, EX-LAX!

MISSED IT!

SOMEDAY I'M GONNA SMASH THAT BALL INTO GARETH'S FACE! THEN *HE'LL* BE THE ONE WHO GETS LAUGHED AT!

BACK IN CLASS.

WHY DO I HAVE TO FIGURE OUT HOW MANY TIMES 25 GOES INTO 450?! WHO CARES? I *HATE* DIVISION!

PTUI!

THWACK!

WHAT HIT ME? SOMETHING SOFT... FEELS SORT OF LIKE...

GUM?

BWA-HA-HA!

THE WAREHOUSE DISTRICT.

HE'S LATE.

THE MEN ARE IN POSITION, *CAPTAIN*.

HE'S *NEVER* LATE.

CAPTAIN RAMSEY, *SIR*, WE HAVE TO MOVE *NOW!* IF WE WAIT ANY LONGER . . .

ALL UNITS BE ADVISED— *DEFENDER* IS ON SCENE!

...A SPECIAL BULLETIN FROM ACTION FIVE NEWS!

STUPID *GARETH BREEDLOVE!* I'D LOVE TO STUFF A FISTFUL OF GUM IN *HIS* HAIR!

COMING TO YOU *LIVE* FROM THE WAREHOUSE DISTRICT, WHERE DEFENDER IS ENTERING A BUILDING ...

WHAT? DEFENDER, *LIVE?!*

...RUMORED TO BE THE HIDEOUT OF THE EVIL MASTERMIND CALLED THE *MAGUS.*

THE MAGUS IS CONSIDERED THE GREATEST AND DEADLIEST—

—*CH!CKEN* YOU'VE EVER TASTED! FIRST WE TENDERIZE THE MEAT, THEN—

CLICK!

BACK AT THE WAREHOUSE.

WHERE ARE THE LIGHTS IN THIS PLACE?

BETTER TREAD CAREFULLY. THE MAGUS IS SURE TO HAVE SET A TRAP....

CLICK!

AH, THERE'S THE SWITCH! NOW, LET'S SEE WHAT KIND OF —

OH, MAMA!

NOT FAR AWAY.

MAYBE DEFENDER WILL MAKE ME HIS *PARTNER!*

HE'LL SEE WHAT I CAN DO—AND THEN I'LL SHOW EVERYONE!

WELL, WELL! IF IT ISN'T OL' BUBBLE HEAD!

WHERE ARE YOU GOING ... ANDREW *CRY-AN?*

NONE OF YOUR BUSINESS!

SCREEE!

IF YOU WANNA GET PAST US, YOU GOTTA PAY THE TOLL!

ONE DOLLAR, WIMP!

HEY! GET BACK HERE!

WHY DON'T YOU JUST SEND ME THE *BILL?*

INSIDE THE WAREHOUSE.

DEFENDER?

WAKEY, WAKEY!

UNH... WHAT? WHERE...?

IT WOULD BE SO RUDE OF YOU TO SLEEP THROUGH MY MOMENT OF GLORY!

IT'S GONNA BE A *SHORT* MOMENT, MAGUS!

NOT THIS TIME, DEAR FELLOW. THAT DEVICE YOU'RE STRAPPED TO IS THE WORK OF MY BEST SCIENTISTS!

IT WILL DRAIN YOUR POWERS AND LEAVE YOU AN EMPTY SHELL...

LIKE A DISCARDED WRAPPER FLUNG IN THE TRASH!

I'VE BEEN SO LOOKING FORWARD TO HARNESSING YOUR POWERS FOR *MYSELF!* FAREWELL, *OLD FRIEND!*

ZZZZZZZTT!

UNGH! IT'S SUCKING... THE LIFE... OUT OF ME!

GOT TO... BREAK... FREE!

SNICK!

NOW, I'LL JUST PULL THIS THING OFF...

HA! TOO EASY—

KA-BOOM!!!

THAT CAN'T BE GOOD.

FOOM!

I'M W-WARNING YOU GUYS. IF YOU GET ME C-CORNERED, I'M LIKE A C-CAGED ANIMAL!

THE FEE FOR RUNNING IS GETTIN' YOUR BUTT KICKED!

HOLY—!

I M-MEAN IT! S-S-STAY *BACK!*

RUN FOR YOUR LIVES!

INSIDE THE WAREHOUSE.

CRACK!

CLEAR!

ALL CLEAR!

ROOM IS SECURE!

ANY SIGN OF DEFENDER? OR THE MAGUS? OR *ANYONE?*

OVER HERE!

THIS COULD BE AN ESCAPE ROUTE . . . IF ANYONE MADE IT OUT ALIVE. . . .

THERE'S *MORE* IN THE NEXT ROOM!

BACK AT THE CONSTRUCTION SITE.

UNH...

FEELS LIKE I TOOK A NAP FOR TEN YEARS!

WHAT IN THE WORLD HIT ME?

THAT'S WEIRD... MY *WRIST*... IT DOESN'T HURT ANYMORE!

WELL, WELL, WELL!

MAN, THIS FEELS *GOOD!* I'M NOT EVEN WINDED—I COULD RUN ALL DAY!

THIS IS TOO MUCH WORK! ≳PANT!≲ LET'S GO PICK ON SOMEONE ELSE!

WHOA! I'M TOO FAST FOR THEM! THAT'S WEIRD...

YIKES!

GOING TOO FAST...!

CAN'T STOP...

TONIGHT, ON A SPECIAL EDITION OF *NEWSLINE*—A TRIBUTE TO THE LATE SUPERHERO, DEFENDER.

HE FIRST APPEARED FIFTEEN YEARS AGO IN AMATEUR FOOTAGE THAT BECAME A GLOBAL SENSATION....

WITH SUPERHUMAN STRENGTH AND THE ABILITY TO FLY, DEFENDER HAD POWERS FAR GREATER THAN ANY *OTHER* COSTUMED HERO.

ALTHOUGH HIS TRUE IDENTITY REMAINS A *SECRET* EVEN IN DEATH, DEFENDER REVEALED HIMSELF TO THE WORLD IN THIS HISTORIC TV INTERVIEW.

FOR THE GOOD OF EVERYONE, I CAN'T DISCUSS *HOW* I GOT THESE POWERS. BUT TRUST ME, THEY'RE *REAL*—AND AWESOME! AND I'LL USE THEM TO FIGHT CRIME UNTIL MY *LAST* BREATH.

SADLY PROPHETIC WORDS. DEFENDER MANIA SWEPT THE WORLD, INSPIRING MANY COPYCATS—THOUGH NONE OF THEM LASTED LONG. STILL, HE WAS NOT WITHOUT CONTROVERSY....

LAW-ENFORCEMENT OFFICIALS, INCLUDING SEATOWN POLICE CAPTAIN *DOUGLAS RAMSEY,* HAVE OBJECTED TO HIS CRIME-FIGHTING ESCAPADES.

DEFENDER'S ARROGANT GRANDSTANDING INTERFERES WITH *REAL* COPS DOING THEIR JOBS. WE'D ALL BE A LOT SAFER IF HE HUNG UP HIS CAPE!

NONETHELESS, HE REMAINS A ROLE MODEL TO *MILLIONS* OF CHILDREN AND ADULTS *ALL OVER THE WORLD.* DEFENDER'S DEATH LEAVES *MANY* UNANSWERED QUESTIONS....

WHO WAS HE? WHO COULD *REPLACE* HIM? AND IS ANYONE ELSE *POWERFUL* ENOUGH TO DEFEAT A CRIMINAL MASTERMIND LIKE THE *MAGUS?*

LATER THAT WEEK.

WHAT MAKES A HERO?

IS IT SOMEONE WHO RISKS *HIS* LIFE SO THAT *OTHERS* MAY LIVE IN PEACE?

IS IT SOMEONE WHO SACRIFICES HIS OWN *WANTS* FOR THE *NEEDS* OF THE WEAK AND HELPLESS?

DEFENDER WAS BOTH OF THESE ... AND MORE. HE WAS THE GREATEST HERO OUR WORLD HAS EVER KNOWN.

AND NOW ... HE IS GONE.

BUT HIS *MEMORY* WILL LIVE ON. AND WE PAY *TRIBUTE* TO HIS LEGACY BY TRYING TO LIVE *OUR* LIVES THE BEST WAY WE CAN.

THAT'S WHAT *HE* WOULD HAVE WANTED ...

DEFENDER GOT RID OF THE DRUG DEALERS IN FRONT OF MY HOUSE. I FELT SAFE LETTING MY SON PLAY ON OUR OWN STOOP. WHO'S GOING TO KEEP US SAFE *NOW?*

SORRY I'M LATE! MY MEETING RAN LONG. DID I MISS MUCH?

ONLY THE EULOGY. NOW PEOPLE ARE SHARING THEIR MEMORIES.

I WROTE A BLOG MAKING FUN OF HIS COSTUME. THEN SOME PUNKS STOLE MY MOST VALUABLE COMICS, AND DEFENDER CAUGHT THEM.

I NEVER GOT TO APOLOGIZE, OR THANK HIM . . .

HOW'S HE DOING, HELEN?

JUST *ASK* HIM, THOMAS.

I'M SORRY ABOUT DEFENDER, BUDDY. DO *YOU* WANT TO GO UP THERE AND SAY SOMETHING?

I DON'T KNOW *WHAT* TO SAY.

I'M *CAPTAIN RAMSEY.* IT'S NO SECRET THAT DEFENDER AND I HAD OUR *DIFFERENCES.* BUT HE SAVED MY LIFE MORE TIMES THAN I CAN COUNT. AND . . . I . . .

I'M SORRY. I HAVE NO WORDS.

SEE YOU NEXT WEEKEND, ANDREW?

HE'LL BE FINE. HE JUST NEEDS TIME.

LATER.

WANT ME TO MAKE YOU A PEANUT-BUTTER-AND-BANANA SANDWICH? IT'S YOUR FAVORITE!

NO, THANKS.

MY GAME'S ON PAUSE, SO DON'T TOUCH IT!

SURE THING.

AND DON'T USE THE PHONE! I'M WAITING FOR A CALL!

NO PROBLEM.

IS ANDREW OK? HE DIDN'T EVEN PUT UP A FIGHT!

HE'S VERY SAD RIGHT NOW, TOMMY.

HEY, ANDREW—I PICKED UP THE NEW DEFENDER COMIC, IF YOU WANT TO READ IT.

COOL, THANKS.

TAKE AS LONG AS YOU WANT. I DON'T NEED IT BACK RIGHT AWAY.

WISH I COULD TELL *SOMEONE* ABOUT MY POWERS.

BUT I CAN'T *TRUST* TOMMY, AND IF I TOLD MOM AND DAD, THEY'D BE SO *WORRIED* THAT THEY WOULDN'T LET ME LEAVE MY ROOM FOR THE REST OF MY LIFE!

WHY DID *I* GET THESE POWERS?

WHAP!

WHY NOT A *COP* LIKE CAPTAIN RAMSEY? OR A *FIREMAN?* OR SOMEONE WHO'S OLD ENOUGH TO *SHAVE?*

I MEAN, WHAT GOOD IS A LITTLE *KID* WHO CAN FLY AND RUN FAST?

BOING!

OH, YEAH— AND HAS SUPER *STRENGTH?*

I DON'T EVEN KNOW *HOW* STRONG I AM!

THUNK!

I'M STILL IN ELEMENTARY SCHOOL.... I CAN'T DRIVE...I CAN'T STAY OUT PAST EIGHT ON A SCHOOL NIGHT!

I COULD *NEVER* BE THE KIND OF HERO YOU WERE!

MEANWHILE...

HE'S BEEN LIKE THIS FOR *DAYS.*

HE DOESN'T SLEEP. WON'T EAT. I'D TRY TALKING TO HIM, BUT I'M AFRAID FOR MY *LIFE.*

BEST LET *ME* HANDLE THIS.

I DON'T KNOW, DOC. HE SAID HE DOESN'T WANT TO BE BOTHERED ...

NOT TO WORRY. I HAVE JUST THE THING TO CHEER HIM UP!

SERIOUSLY, I DON'T THINK NOW'S A GOOD—

MAGUS, OLD CHUM! YOUR LONGTIME ENEMY IS FINALLY BEATEN! LET'S CELEBRATE!

TELL ME SOMETHING, DR. WILSON ...

POP!

I STILL HAVE THAT *COSTUME* MOM MADE ME FOR *HALLOWEEN!*

WHERE IS IT? IT'S GOTTA BE... *AHA!*

WHAP!

OUCH!

HEY, BRO! WANNA MAKE COOKIES? I BOUGHT SOME FROZEN CHOCOLATE-CHIP COOKIE DOUGH...

ANDREW?

THIS MIGHT BE THE CRAZIEST, DUMBEST THING I'VE EVER DONE!

BUT IF I REALLY DO HAVE DEFENDER'S POWERS... I GUESS IT'S UP TO ME TO USE THEM FOR GOOD!

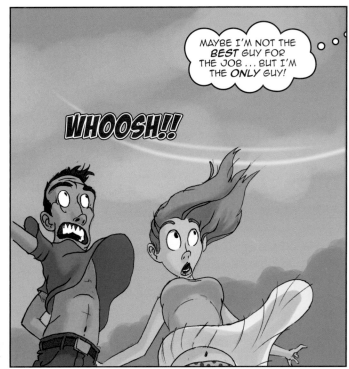

MAYBE I'M NOT THE BEST GUY FOR THE JOB... BUT I'M THE ONLY GUY!

WHOOSH!!

...BANK ROBBERS?

IT'S JUST A... KID?

HELLO, LITTLE MAN! HOW'D YOU GET IN HERE?

I WAS, UM, H-HIDING FROM MY *MOM* ON THE ROOF! I *SLIPPED* A—AND FELL THROUGH THE WINDOW!

I SAY *SHOOT* HIM, TO BE *SAFE!*

HE'S JUST A KID, YOU NINNY!

PUT HIM WITH THE *OTHERS* FOR NOW.

WELL, *THIS* DIDN'T WORK OUT LIKE I'D PLANNED!

WONDER IF *DEFENDER* STARTED OUT LIKE THIS!

I DON'T *LIKE* THIS. HE COULD BE A *COP!*

THE POLICE ACADEMY'S GOT A *KINDERGARTEN* NOW?

RELAX, THE EXPLOSIVES ARE SET.

YOU PUSH THE BUTTON AND IT ALL GOES *BOOM!*

THIS WAY, KID!

SWEET, *SASSY* CRAP!

THESE GUYS HAVE MORE EXPLOSIVES THAN *WILE E. COYOTE!*

NOT *ANOTHER* ONE!

IT'S A LITTLE *KID!*

WHERE DID *HE* COME FROM?!

HERE YA GO, BRAT. GET COMFY.

IT'S OK. YOU'RE SAFE HERE WITH US!

I'VE GOTTA GET THESE PEOPLE OUT OF HERE . . .

SAFE? THOSE GOONS WILL LET US GO OVER THEIR DEAD BODIES!

DON'T SAY THAT. YOU'LL SCARE HIM!

HEY, UH . . . WHERE DOES THAT *VENT* GO?

THAT'S THE COPS... RIGHT ON SCHEDULE!

BZZZZZT!

BANK ROBBER SPEAKING. WHO'S CALLING, PLEASE?

THIS IS **CAPTAIN RAMSEY** OF THE SEATOWN POLICE DEPARTMENT. LET THE HOSTAGES GO, AND WE'LL DISCUSS YOUR DEMANDS.

I WANT **ALL** COPS CLEARED OUT IN ONE HOUR, INCLUDING THOSE **SNIPERS** ON THE ROOFTOPS!

BUT THE HOSTAGES— HELLO? **HELLO?**

HE HUNG UP.

SIR! SNIPERS SAW THE PERSON WHO FLEW THROUGH THAT WINDOW! THEY SAID IT LOOKED...

LIKE **DEFENDER!**

WE CAN ONLY PRAY IT'S HIM.

NOT ANOTHER STEP OR IT'S BYE-BYE, *PUBERTY!*

IT WAS AN *ACCIDENT,* I SWEAR!

STEP AWAY *SLOWLY....*

NO, WAIT. *STOP!* DON'T TAKE ANOTHER—

CRUNCH!

—STEP!

DEET! DEET!

BEEEEEEEEP!

BA-DA-DOOM!!

THINGS KEEP BLOWIN' UP AROUND HERE!

LATER THAT NIGHT.

CHANNEL FOUR SPOKE TO WITNESSES WHO SAW THE COSTUMED HERO IN *ACTION!*

THIS KID IN HIS JAMMIES FLIES RIGHT PAST ME AND—*SMASH!* HITS A STEEL *GIRDER.*

I'M ALL LIKE, "WAY TO GO, *SMASH!*" HAW–HAW!

THAT OUGHTA BE HIS NAME... *SMASH!* HAW–HAW!

THAT'S *ME* THEY'RE TALKING ABOUT! I'M *FAMOUS!*

I'M *COOL* ...

STUPID *JERK!* IF YOU SNEAK OUT AND GET HURT, *I* GET BUSTED!

SORRY, TOMMY! I DIDN'T MEAN TO—

IF MOM FINDS OUT AND I GET GROUNDED, *I* SWEAR ...

WHAT ARE YOU TWO DOING UP? IT'S *MIDNIGHT!*

GET TO BED RIGHT NOW, *BOTH* OF YOU— OR NO TV FOR A *WEEK!*

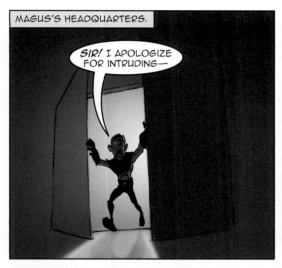

SIR! I APOLOGIZE FOR INTRUDING—

. . . BUT YOU *HAVE* TO SEE WHAT'S ON THE NEWS.

. . . HOSTAGE SITUATION WAS APPARENTLY FOILED BY *THIS* UNNAMED FIGURE.

THE HOSTAGES TELL A *REMARKABLE* STORY OF COURAGE . . .

THIS *LITTLE BOY* IN HIS PAJAMAS FLEW US UP TO A VENT! THANKS TO *HIM,* WE ALL GOT OUT BEFORE THE BOMB WENT OFF!

POLICE OFFICIALS ARE *BAFFLED* BY THE INCIDENT AND CLAIM THEY KNOW *NOTHING* ABOUT THE YOUNG HERO . . .

I WANT TO SEE *DR. COBB.*

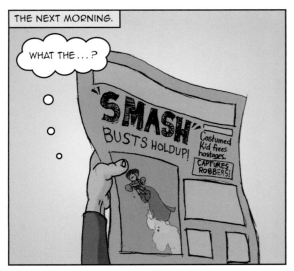

THE NEXT MORNING.

WHAT THE...?

'SMASH' BUSTS HOLDUP! Costumed kid frees hostages. CAPTURES ROBBERS!

I COME UP WITH A COOL NAME LIKE *SPARROWHAWK*— AND THE PRESS CALLS ME "SMASH"!

LATER.

NONE OF THESE KIDS HAS ANY *IDEA* THERE'S A *HERO* SITTING AMONG THEM!

AT RECESS.

CAN'T CATCH ME, MAGUS!

I WANNA BE *SMASH* THIS TIME!

EVERYONE WANTS TO *BE* ME!

HEADS UP!

WHANG!

NOWHERE TO *RUN* THIS TIME, *WIMP*!

LET'S FINISH WHAT WE STARTED!

TIME TO GET POUNDED!

WHAT'S GOING *ON* HERE? SAVE IT FOR P.E. CLASS, *BREEDLOVE!*

YOU BOYS SEEM INCAPABLE OF KEEPING YOUR HANDS TO YOURSELVES.

I DIDN'T DO ANYTHING! *ANDREW* STARTED IT!

SOMEHOW, I *DOUBT* THAT. LET'S SEE IF YOUR PARENTS BELIEVE YOU!

ANDREW, ARE YOU ALL RIGHT?

DON'T CALL MY MOM! I BEG YOU!

SAVE IT, TOUGH GUY!

YEAH, I FEEL *GREAT!* UH, I MEAN, IT DOESN'T HURT *TOO* MUCH ...

YOU *REALLY* STOOD UP TO GARETH!

I WAS ROOTING FOR *YOU* THE WHOLE TIME!

WAY TO *GO,* ANDREW!

WHO KNEW I COULD *WIN* WITHOUT EVEN *FIGHTING?*

LATER.

FEELS *STRANGE* ... LIKE I DON'T HAVE TO BE SCARED OF *ANYTHING,* EVER AGAIN!

AND NOW, A LOOK AT *SMASH!* SOME SAY HE'S ONLY A CHILD AND SHOULD BE STOPPED BEFORE HE HURTS HIMSELF...

AW, C'MON!— *SMASH?*

WHILE OTHER EXPERTS MAINTAIN HE'S JUST A *VERY SHORT* PERSON...

HEY! WHERE ARE *YOU* GOING THIS LATE, TOMMY?

MOM SAID YOU'RE *GROUNDED!* PLUS, YOU'RE NOT SUPPOSED TO GO *OUT* ON SCHOOL NIGHTS.

SHUT UP, YOU LITTLE *JERK!* YOU AREN'T THE BOSS OF ME—*NOBODY* IS!

AND IT'S *TOM*, NOT *TOMMY!* GOT IT?

SLAM!

OOOOOOKAAAAY... *THAT* WAS *INTENSE!*

MOMENTS LATER.

MOM will get off work in an HOUR, so I can't stay out too late...

BUT I HAVE TO FIND OUT WHERE TOMMY'S GOING! I MEAN... TOM.

I HAVE TO MAKE SURE HE STAYS OUT OF TROUBLE.

HEY, IF HE DOES GET INTO TROUBLE, I COULD RESCUE HIM. THAT'D BE PRETTY COOL!

WHO ARE THOSE GUYS? OH, YEAH... HIS JERK FRIENDS!

WHY DOES HE HANG OUT WITH PUNKS LIKE THAT? I SHOULD FLY DOWN AND GIVE THEM A SCARE—

BOOM!

WHAT THE—?

THUD!

OK, *THAT* HURT.

MAYBE IT'S A LITTLE SOON FOR ME TO TACKLE A TRIO OF *ROBOTS!* I'LL COME BACK WHEN I'VE HAD SOME MORE—

OH, DON'T DO IT!

POPPAPOPPAPOPPAPOPPAPOPPAPOPPA

YAAAAAAHHHH!

WELL, *THIS* STINKS!

FIRST, TAKE OUT THE *MACHINE GUN!* THEN, IF I'M NOT *DEAD*, WORRY ABOUT THE OTHER TWO!

KUNG!

CRIPES, I'M *STUCK!* GIVE ME BACK MY HAND, YOU METAL *FREAK!*

UH-OH!

RRRRAAAAGH!

POPPAPOPPAPOPPAPOPPAPOPPA

PING!

PING!

PING!

PING!

PING!

PING!

HOW DO I SHUT THIS GUN OFF?

POPPAPOPPAPOPPAPOPPAPOPPAPOPPAPOPPAPOP

POPPAPOPPAPOPPA

SHUNK!

THERE!

BACK TO THE SCRAP HEAP!

THE RYANS' HOUSE.

MOM, CAN YOU PATCH UP MY DEFENDER COSTUME?

I, UH, *FELL DOWN* AND IT GOT A LITTLE RIPPED.

IT'S *RUINED!* WE SHOULD THROW IT OUT. I CAN MAKE YOU A *NEW COSTUME* NEXT YEAR—

JUST SEW THIS ONE UP. IT'LL BE *FINE!*

ANDREW! YOU—YOU'RE *SMASH?*

HEH, HEH! C'MON, TOM, YOU'RE TALKING LIKE A *LOONY!*

ALSO, HIS NAME *ISN'T* SMASH, IT'S SPARROWHAWK! AND I'M DEFINITELY *NOT* HIM!

YOUNG MAN, YOU ARE *GROUNDED!* NO FIGHTING CRIME FOR A *WEEK!* AND NO TV, EITHER!

NOOOOOOOOOOOOOOOOOOOO!

ANDREW! ARE YOU ALL RIGHT?

THAT MUST HAVE BEEN SOME NIGHTMARE!

IT SEEMED SO *REAL*...

WELL, YOU'RE OK NOW. DO YOU REMEMBER WHAT IT WAS ABOUT?

UH... I FORGET. I'M JUST GLAD YOU'RE— I MEAN, *I'M* SAFE!

TRY TO GO BACK TO SLEEP, HONEY. WHERE'S THAT COSTUME YOU WANTED ME TO MEND?

COSTUME? *WHAT* COSTUME? HEY, WOULDJA LOOK AT THE *TIME*, I BETTER GET SOME *Z'S!* *NUH-NIGHT,* MOM!

UH, OK. SWEET DREAMS...?

÷WHEW!÷ CLOSE ONE! I'D BETTER FIGURE OUT HOW TO SEW...

LAB OF DR. COBB.

OH, BABY!

FOOM!!

FEEL THAT POWER! NOW THAT'S WHAT I'M TALKIN' ABOUT!

ABOUT MY FEE, MISTER—

JUST CALL ME PULSE!

THESE BLASTERS ARE GREAT, COBB! WORTH EVERY PENNY!

FOR ANOTHER FIFTY THOUSAND, I OFFER A FULL FIVE-YEAR WARRANTY...

WHOA! WHAT'S WITH HIM?

EASY, BRUTE.

IT SEEMS WE HAVE... UNEXPECTED COMPANY.

I WILL, OF COURSE, PAY *HANDSOMELY* FOR IT!

IF AT FIRST YOU DON'T *SUCCEED,* EH? AN *INTRIGUING* PROPOSITION . . .

VERY WELL. I *ACCEPT* YOUR OFFER.

ONE MORE THING, COBB. I'M *NOT* BUYING A *WARRANTY.* MAKE SURE IT WORKS RIGHT THE *FIRST* TIME!

DISAPPOINT ME . . .

AND EVEN YOUR *GORILLA* WON'T BE ABLE TO SAVE YOU!

POLICE HEADQUARTERS.

EXCUSE ME, CAPTAIN RAMSEY...

IT'S *LATE*, DETECTIVE DORIX. WHAT DO YOU *NEED?*

ACTUALLY, SIR, IT'S PRONOUNCED DOOR-*OH*.

OR DOOR-*OOH*, IF YOU PREFER THE *FRENCH*—

DID YOU COME IN HERE TO TELL ME HOW TO SAY YOUR *NAME?*

NO, SIR. I'M WRITING MY *REPORT* ON THE DEFENDER CASE...

SERGEANT HALSEY HEARD YOU TELL *DEFENDER* THAT YOU HAVE A "MAN ON THE INSIDE." IF THERE'S A *COP* WORKING *UNDERCOVER* AS A MINION...

I'D LIKE TO *TALK* TO HIM ABOUT HIS TIP ON THE MAGUS.

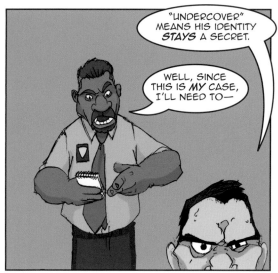

"UNDERCOVER" MEANS HIS IDENTITY **STAYS** A SECRET.

WELL, SINCE THIS IS **MY** CASE, I'LL NEED TO—

THE CASE IS **CLOSED**, DETECTIVE!

DEFENDER IS **DEAD**. THE MAGUS **KILLED** HIM. **END** OF STORY! GOT IT?

YEAH, CAPTAIN. I **GOT** IT.

STUPID, NOSY **DETECTIVES!**

ALWAYS **SNIFFING** AROUND . . .

JUST LIKE **I** USED TO!

DOUROUX'S LIKE A **SHARK** THAT SMELLS BLOOD. HE **WON'T** LET UP, NO MATTER **HOW** MUCH I—

EXCUSE ME, CAPTAIN . . .

MIGHT I HAVE A **WORD** WITH YOU?

ARE YOU *CRAZY,* COMING HERE?! SOMEONE MIGHT *SEE* US!

THEN I SUGGEST YOU GET *IN.*

I THOUGHT OUR DEAL WAS FINISHED! YOU *GOT* WHAT YOU WANTED.

I'M AFRAID NOT. IT SEEMS DEFENDER'S POWERS HAVE FOUND A NEW HOME—NOT IN *ME,* BUT IN THE BODY OF A *CHILD!*

THIS IS *UNACCEPTABLE.*

NOT *MY* PROBLEM, MAGUS! *YOU* BOTCHED YOUR LITTLE SCIENCE PROJECT, NOT *ME!* YOU WANTED ME TO DELIVER DEFENDER TO YOU, AND I DID.

I DIDN'T COME HERE TO *ARGUE* WITH YOU, RAMSEY. I CAME TO *CONVINCE* YOU.

WHAT IS THIS?

DEFENDER HAS BEEN A THORN IN **BOTH** OUR SIDES FOR TOO LONG. IF YOU **HELP** ME, I GUARANTEE YOU CAN GO ON LIVING A HAPPY, PEACEFUL LIFE AS A POLICE CAPTAIN.

ARE YOU **THREATENING** ME, MAGUS?

WHY, NOTHING OF THE SORT! I'M MERELY CONCERNED FOR THE **SAFETY** OF YOUR ADORABLE **FAMILY.**

I ASSURE YOU, MY **ONLY** INTEREST IS IN TAKING DEFENDER'S POWERS.

AND ONCE THIS MATTER IS **CLOSED,** YOU WON'T HEAR FROM ME AGAIN.

WHATEVER IT TAKES, MAGUS!

I'M CURIOUS HOW MANY HITS THIS VIDEO WOULD GET ONLINE. I THINK IT MIGHT GO **VIRAL.**

WE HAVE COPIES READY TO SEND TO LOCAL NEWS STATIONS. THE DIGITAL REPRODUCTION IS **SUPERB!**

WHAT DO **YOU** THINK?

I'LL BE IN TOUCH . . .

DEAR GOD . . . WHAT HAVE I **DONE?**

MEANWHILE...

GOTTA GET OVER MY *FEAR OF HEIGHTS* IF I'M GOING TO BE ANY KIND OF *SUPERHERO*.

I FLEW UP *FOUR* FLOORS, SO *TWENTY* MORE SHOULDN'T BE A BIG DEAL...RIGHT?

EVEN THOUGH IT'S SUCH A *LOOOOONG* WAY TO FALL...

ALL RIGHT! NO *GUTS*, NO GLORY! IT'S *FLYIN'* TIME!

ON *THREE!* ONE, TWO...OK, *WAIT.* EENIE, MEENIE, MINEY...NO, THAT'S NO GOOD. OK... HERE IT *COMES*...

AAAAAAND... AWAY... WE...

GO!

DON'T LOOK DOWN! DON'T EVEN *THINK* ABOUT WHAT'S *NOT* UNDER YOU!

"I STARTED IN THE '60S. USING *ATOMIC-AGE SCIENCE*, I DESIGNED A *SUIT* THAT WOULD ENABLE ME TO *PHASE* THROUGH ANY SURFACE AND *MATERIALIZE* ON THE OTHER SIDE!"

"AS MY CAREER CONTINUED INTO THE '70S, I DEVELOPED A *NOTORIOUS* ROGUES' GALLERY, INCLUDING *MAN-CAT*, *MIRRORBALL*, AND THE *ROLLER TWINS!*"

"BY THE LATE '80S, *ALL* OF THEM WERE RETIRED OR IN PRISON. THE *LUCKY* ONES, ANYWAY. AS TIMES CHANGED, THERE SEEMED LESS OF A NEED FOR SOMEONE LIKE *ME* TO FIGHT CRIME."

WAAAAIT, I READ ABOUT YOU! YOU FOUGHT *DEFENDER* BACK IN THE '90S! MAN, HE KICKED YOUR BUTT . . .

IT WAS A SIMPLE MISUNDERSTANDING CAUSED BY THE MAGUS!

"ONCE WE FIGURED OUT WE'D BEEN DUPED, WE *TEAMED UP* AND STOPPED THE MAGUS FROM UNLEASHING AN ARMY OF ROBOTIC SOLDIERS!"

"WHEN I SAW HOW CAPABLY HE DEALT WITH THE MAGUS, IT WAS CLEAR THAT DEFENDER DIDN'T NEED *MY* HELP. SO I *RETIRED* AND STARTED A DOGGIE DAY CARE."

BUT NOW, HE'S GONE... AND I'M NEEDED AGAIN.

NO WORRIES, *OLD-TIMER...*

I'M HERE TO PICK UP WHERE DEFENDER LEFT OFF!

YOU'RE *TOO YOUNG.*

WHADDAYA MEAN, "TOO YOUNG"? HAVE YOU *SEEN* WHAT I CAN *DO?*

YEAH, I'VE SEEN YOU FLY AROUND AND SMASH INTO THINGS. YOU NEED *TRAINING* AND *EXPERIENCE.* WE'LL START YOU AS MY *SIDEKICK* SO YOU CAN STUDY MY MOVES —

NO WAY! SIDEKICKS *SPEW!* BESIDES, YOU'RE TOO *OLD* TO TEACH *ME* ANYTHING!

OH, YOU THINK SO? WELL ...

WE DON'T KNOW *HOW* IT HAPPENED, BUT THE BOY *DEFINITELY* HAS DEFENDER'S POWERS.

THOUGH NOT HIS SKILLS OR STRENGTH . . . *YET.*

THEIR ENERGY IMPRINTS ARE AN *EXACT MATCH,* SIR.

PITY HE WON'T LIVE LONG ENOUGH TO *DEVELOP* THOSE SKILLS!

IF WE MEASURE THE *FORCE* OF DEFENDER'S BLOWS BY POUNDS PER SQUARE INCH, OR *PSI* . . .

SINCE *FORCE* IS EQUAL TO MASS TIMES ACCELERATION, AND ONE *POUND* IS ROUGHLY EQUAL TO 4.5 *NEWTONS*—

IN *ENGLISH,* PLEASE

DEFENDER'S PUNCHES INITIALLY CLOCKED IN AT *600* PSI. BY THE TIME HE MET HIS *DEMISE,* THAT NUMBER HAD GONE UP TO *1,000* PSI.

IF DEFENDER'S POWERS *INCREASED* OVER TIME, IT STANDS TO REASON THAT *SMASH'S* WILL, AS WELL.

THE RYANS' HOUSE.

HOW DOES IT FEEL TO BE THE *FIRST* CRIMINAL APPREHENDED BY *SMASH?*

FASCINATING. WHEN WE COME BACK . . .

WHEN I GET OUTTA HERE, I'LL *SHOW* THAT SNOT-NOSED BRAT—

NO COMMENT!

MY CLIENT IS *INNOCENT!* SHUT THAT THING *OFF!*

ARE YOU BOTH PACKED? YOUR *FATHER'S* HERE, SO GET YOUR BAGS.

I'M *NOT* GOING TO DAD'S *STUPID* APARTMENT!

IT'S HIS WEEKEND TO SEE YOU, TOMMY. GET *BACK* HERE!

I DON'T CARE! THERE'S A PARTY TOMORROW NIGHT AND I'M *NOT* MISSING IT TO HANG OUT WITH *DAD!*

AND MY NAME'S *TOM,* NOT TOMMY! I'M NOT A BABY ANYMORE!

HEY, *BIG GUY!* HOW 'BOUT A *HUG?*

DROP DEAD.

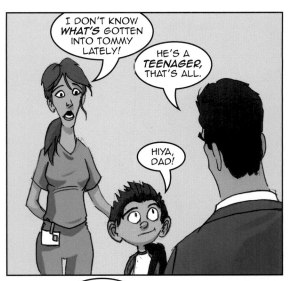

I DON'T KNOW *WHAT'S* GOTTEN INTO TOMMY LATELY!

HE'S A *TEENAGER,* THAT'S ALL.

HIYA, DAD!

I PACKED MY COSTUME, IN CASE I CAN SNEAK AWAY TO USE IT. TOO BAD DAD DOESN'T WORK *NIGHTS* LIKE MOM DOES!

WHO WANTS *ICE CREAM?*

SOUNDS GREAT!

HOW'S SCHOOL?

GOOD.

HOW'S YOUR MOM?

GOOD.

HOW'S YOUR ICE CREAM?

GOOD.

RING! RING!

THE ICE-CREAM PARLOR.

C'MON, DAD, YOU'VE *GOTTA* BE OK! CAN YOU HEAR ME? *SAY* SOMETHING!

OVER HERE! MAN DOWN!

PLEASE, GIVE US SOME ROOM! IS THAT YOUR FATHER?

Y-YEAH... IS HE GONNA *LIVE*?

I'VE GOT A PULSE!

LISTEN TO ME. WE'RE TAKING YOUR DAD TO THE HOSPITAL. WE'LL TAKE CARE OF HIM—I *PROMISE*!

EVEN WITH ALL MY NEW POWERS, I COULDN'T PROTECT MY OWN *DAD*!

WHERE'D THAT KID GO?

BUT I *CAN* MAKE WHOEVER DID THIS *SORRY* HE WAS EVER BORN!

EAGLE ONE TO *NEST!* I'M IN POSITION!

HAVE YOU GOT HIM IN YOUR SIGHTS?

JUST ABOUT...

THERE HE IS!

WUH-OH!

FOOM!

WHO *ELSE* WANTS A TASTE? C'MON, COPS, IS THAT ALL YOU GOT?

GEEZ, THAT COP WAS SUCH A JERK!

BET NOBODY TRIED TO ARREST *DEFENDER* FOR BEING A HERO!

DAD'S GOTTA BE AROUND HERE *SOMEWHERE.*

ACT LIKE YOU *KNOW* WHERE YOU'RE GOING... NO ONE WILL *NOTICE* YOU...

I'VE GOT K-9 UNITS *AND* PATROL CARS SCOURING THE AREA. DON'T WORRY, WE'LL FIND—

MOM? DAD?

THERE HE IS! I *TOLD* YOU HE'D TURN UP!

ANDREW?

WE WERE *SO* WORRIED—NO ONE COULD *FIND* YOU! ARE YOU *HURT?*

I'M FINE! I GOT SCARED AND HID UNTIL THE COAST WAS CLEAR.

H-HOW ARE *YOU*, DAD? ARE YOU HURT REALLY BAD?

I GOT A FEW *DINGS*, BUT IT *LOOKS* WORSE THAN IT IS. I'LL BE BACK ON MY FEET IN *NO* TIME!

I'M JUST GLAD *YOU'RE* ALL RIGHT.

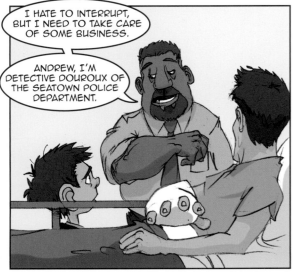

I HATE TO INTERRUPT, BUT I NEED TO TAKE CARE OF SOME BUSINESS.

ANDREW, I'M DETECTIVE DOUROUX OF THE SEATOWN POLICE DEPARTMENT.

AM—AM I UNDER ARREST?

DON'T BE SILLY, HONEY! WHAT WOULD MAKE YOU THINK THAT?

I JUST NEED TO ASK A FEW *QUESTIONS* ABOUT WHAT YOU SAW TODAY.

HOSPITAL CAFETERIA.

AND FROM WHERE YOU WERE HIDING, YOU COULDN'T SEE ANYTHING ELSE?

NOPE—I HAD MY EYES COVERED MOST OF THE TIME. SORRY...

NO NEED TO APOLOGIZE, ANDREW. YOU'VE BEEN VERY HELPFUL. WE'LL CATCH THIS "SMASH" CHARACTER ONE WAY OR ANOTHER!

HE DOESN'T *SEEM* LIKE A BAD GUY! AND I THINK HIS *REAL* NAME IS SPARROW—

DO YOU *REALLY* THINK SMASH IS A LITTLE KID?

DON'T SEE HOW HE COULD BE. IT'S PROBABLY ANOTHER TRICK CREATED BY THE MAGUS. IF YOU THINK OF ANYTHING ELSE, GIVE ME A *CALL*.

÷WHEW!÷ THAT WAS CLOSE. I THOUGHT HE FIGURED ME OUT FOR SURE!

I HAVE TO GO BACK TO WORK, ANDREW. DO YOU FEEL OK TAKING THE *BUS* HOME?

A SHORT WHILE LATER.

GUESS THERE'S NO USE FIGHTING IT. EVERYONE'S CALLING ME *SMASH*, WHETHER I LIKE IT OR NOT!

WHUP! WHUP! WHUP!

WHUP! WHUP! WHUP!

HOLD IT RIGHT THERE, *SMASH!*

NOT *AGAIN!* CAN'T YOU COPS GIVE IT A *REST?!*

EASY, KID! YOU'RE NOT IN DANGER!

I HAD AN ARRANGEMENT WITH DEFENDER THAT I COULD CONTACT HIM WHENEVER THERE'S *TROUBLE.*

TAKE THIS— IT'S A *SPECIAL* PHONE.

CAN WE CALL *YOU* NOW WHEN WE NEED HELP?

COOL! IT'S NOT EXACTLY THE BAT SIGNAL... BUT IT'LL WORK!

THANKS, CAPTAIN RAMSEY!

SEE YA AROUND!

YEAH... SEE YOU.

WHUP!
WHUP!
WHUP!
WHUP!

I SHOULD STUDY FOR THAT TEST ON MONDAY, BUT I'M **BEAT!** STILL... IF I DON'T PASS, I'LL BE **GROUNDED!**

FOUND YOU...

MONDAY MORNING.

UGH. FEELS LIKE I **SLEPT** THE WHOLE WEEKEND! AND I'M **STILL** TIRED!

AND I NEVER DID STUDY! BETTER CRAM DURING RECESS...

EXCUSE ME, YOUNG MAN...

CAN I HELP YOU?

I JUST WANTED TO SEE WHAT **SMASH** REALLY LOOKS LIKE!

WHAT'S THE BIG IDEA, SCARING ME LIKE THAT?! HOW DID YOU FIND ME?

FIRST RULE OF BEING A HERO: IF YOU WANT YOUR SECRET IDENTITY TO *STAY SECRET, DON'T* FLY HOME WEARING YOUR *COSTUME!*

YOU WERE SO *EASY* TO FOLLOW—

WHAT, ARE YOU *STALKING* ME NOW?

YOU NEED TRAINING! HERE'S MY CARD—

I DON'T WANT YOUR STUPID CARD! TRAIN *YOURSELF* TO STOP BEING A *CREEP!*

I'M GONNA BE LATE FOR SCHOOL.

TAKE THE CARD ANYWAY— JUST IN CASE!

LEAVE ME ALONE, MISTER STRANGER! I DON'T *WANNA* RIDE IN YOUR *VAN!*

HEH, HEH . . . HE WAS KIDDING. REALLY! WE'RE OLD *FRIENDS.*

ELSEWHERE.

DR. COBB HAS EXCEEDED MY EXPECTATIONS.

I'M PLEASED HE FINISHED EARLY. THE QUESTION IS, DOES IT *WORK?*

IT ALL *SEEMS* FUNCTIONAL ... THOUGH, OF COURSE, WE HAVE NO WAY TO *TEST* IT.

NOT TRUE. THE DEVICE IS ABOUT TO HAVE ITS ONE AND *ONLY* TEST.

POLICE HEADQUARTERS.

BZZT! BZZT!

NOW WHAT?

RAMSEY HERE.

DO YOU RECOGNIZE MY VOICE?

THE TIME HAS COME TO *BAIT* THE *TRAP.* DO IT NOW.

AT SCHOOL.

WISH I'D **STUDIED** THIS WEEKEND!

STUPID **PULSE** AND HIS STUPID **ROBBERY!**

WHUNG!

WHAT THE . . . ?

NICE REFLEXES, BOOKWORM!

WHAT'S THE MATTER? **MOMMY** WON'T LET YOU **PLAY** WITH OTHER KIDS?

HEARD YOUR DAD GOT BEAT UP BY THAT LAME **PULSE** GUY. GUESS YOUR WHOLE **FAMILY'S** A BUNCH OF **WIMPS!**

THAT **DOES** IT! YOU WANT A FIGHT, GARETH? YOU'RE GONNA **GET—**

UH . . . **'SCUSE** ME A SEC!

BZZT!

BZZT!

H-HELLO? UH, I MEAN, ÷AHEM!÷ *SMASH SPEAKING!*

WE'VE CORNERED A MINION INSIDE THE OLD FIREHOUSE ON FIFTH AND MAIN.

NOW? CAN IT WAIT TILL THREE?

CRIME DOESN'T HAPPEN ON *YOUR SCHEDULE!* IF YOU WANNA TAKE OVER FOR *DEFENDER*—

OK, *OK!* I'M ON MY WAY!

I'LL THINK UP AN EXCUSE LATER. RIGHT NOW I NEED A *DIVERSION....*

IT'S *MINE,* GARETH! GIVE IT BACK!

ALL YOU GOTTA DO IS *TAKE* IT, SHRIMP!

KUNG!

AWESOME SHOT!

GARETH! SPEAK TO ME!

POOM!

POOM!

NETS? IT'S A *TRAP!*

÷WHEW!÷ SOMETIMES IT PAYS TO BE SMALL!

BLAZES! THE NETS WERE DESIGNED FOR *DEFENDER!* THEY'RE TOO *BIG* FOR THAT LITTLE PIMPLE!

UH, WHOOPS....

SECOND WAVE, *GO!*

YES, SIR!

OUR TURN!

"MANY YEARS AGO, I WAS ONE OF A DOZEN TEST SUBJECTS IN AN EXPERIMENT TO EXPAND THE BOUNDARIES OF HUMAN ENDURANCE. I TRAINED RIGOROUSLY—*OBSESSIVELY*— TO BECOME THE TOP CANDIDATE IN THE PROGRAM."

"SADLY, MY MOMENT OF GLORY WAS *STOLEN* BY MY CLOSEST COMPETITOR! I COULDN'T *PROVE* IT, BUT I KNOW HE *CHEATED* TO WIN THE TOP SPOT!"

"DURING THE EXPERIMENT, THE MACHINE SOMEHOW *MALFUNCTIONED*. THE EXPLOSION *BOMBARDED* HIM WITH ENERGY THAT GAVE HIM SUPERHUMAN STRENGTH AND THE ABILITY TO FLY."

"YES, THAT'S RIGHT... HE BECAME *DEFENDER!* USING POWERS THAT SHOULD HAVE BEEN *MINE!*"

"WHEN THE LAB WAS REBUILT, I FINALLY HAD *MY CHANCE!* HOWEVER, NO MATTER HOW HARD THEY TRIED, THE SCIENTISTS COULD NEVER DUPLICATE THE ACCIDENT."

"WHILE MY SIZE AND STRENGTH WERE INCREASED BEYOND THAT OF A NORMAL HUMAN, THEY'RE *NOTHING* COMPARED TO DEFENDER'S ABILITIES!"

BUT NOW, AT LONG LAST, I SHALL CLAIM WHAT WAS RIGHTFULLY *MINE!*

I ASSURE YOU, THIS WILL GO *MUCH* EASIER IF YOU DON'T RESIST. THAT'S WHAT COST *DEFENDER* HIS *LIFE!*

POLICE HEADQUARTERS.

RIGHT NOW YOU'RE LOOKIN' AT A *LIFETIME* IN PRISON! BUT IF YOU TELL US WHERE MAGUS IS HOLDING SMASH, I'LL TALK TO THE *DA* ABOUT A DEAL—

UH, DETECTIVE *DOUROUX?*

IT'S BEEN AN *HOUR* AND HE HASN'T SAID *SQUAT!* I DON'T THINK HE'S GONNA TALK.

MAYBE I'M ASKING THE WRONG GUY.

CAPTAIN RAMSEY!

SPLURK!

IF YOU'VE GOT A *MAN* ON THE INSIDE, CALL HIM—*NOW*—AND FIND OUT WHERE THE MAGUS IS!

FIRST OFF, I DON'T ANSWER TO *YOU!* AND *SECOND*—

SAVE IT! A BOY'S LIFE IS AT STAKE! WE'VE GOTTA MOVE *NOW!*

GET OUT OF MY OFFICE WHILE YOU STILL HAVE A *BADGE.*

IF ANYTHING HAPPENS TO THAT KID, I'M HOLDING YOU RESPONSIBLE . . . *CAPTAIN!*

THE OLD FIREHOUSE.

ONLY TWO MINIONS! BETTER MAKE MY MOVE BEFORE *OTHERS* SHOW UP!

INITIATE *PRE-ACTIVATION* SEQUENCE!

INITIATING!

EVERYONE HAS THOSE *KEYS* AROUND THEIR NECKS!

I THINK *I* SHOULD GET ONE, TOO!

NICE AND *SLOW*. *EASY* DOES IT . . .

ALMOOOOST GOT IIIIIIIIIIIT . . .

WHAT THE?

WHAP!

BOOM!

KERR-ESH!

THE PROCEDURE WAS *INTERRUPTED!* QUICK, *ALERT* THE MAGUS—

THAT SMARTED!

HOLY MAMA!

FWUMP!

WHOOSH!

I FEEL SO WEIRD, LIKE I'M NOT ALL HERE! WHAT'D THEY *DO* TO ME?

GOTTA *PULL* MYSELF TOGETHER AND GET *MOVING* BEFORE...

PLAYTIME'S OVER, BOY!

WHUMP!

EITHER HE'S **STRONGER** THAN I THOUGHT, OR I'VE GOTTEN A LOT **WEAKER!**

I AM **NOT** AMUSED!

‡HUUKK!‡ YEAH, I CAN SEE THAT!

IT OCCURS TO ME I DON'T NEED YOU **ALIVE** TO DRAIN YOUR POWERS!

CAN'T GO **RIGHT** . . . CAN'T GO **LEFT** . . . CAN'T REACH THE **VENT!** LOOKS LIKE THE **ONLY** WAY OUT IS . . .

UP.

YOU **WANT** THESE POWERS, MAGUS?

‡HURK!‡ LET'S SEE HOW **BAD!**

WHAT ARE YOU DOING? STOP, YOU FOOL!

LATER.

SIR, THE TUNNELS ARE *EMPTY!* THE DIVERS HAVEN'T FOUND A BODY...

KEEP LOOKING. WE'LL SCOUR THE OCEAN FLOOR, IF NECESSARY! WHATEVER IT TAKES... WE *WILL* FIND THAT *BOY!*

MEANWHILE...

WITNESSES REPORTED SEEING THE MAGUS STRUGGLING WITH A FIGURE WHO APPEARED TO BE *SMASH*...

CAUSING INCREDIBLE DAMAGE TO THE FIREHOUSE.

DING-DONG!

WHO JUST *DROPS BY* THIS LATE?

IF IT'S AN OLD VILLAIN LOOKING TO SETTLE SOME SCORE, HE'S IN FOR A *REAL—*

145